Illustrated by Steve Lambe

 A GOLDEN BOOK · NEW YORK

© 2016 Viacom International Inc. and Viacom Overseas Holdings C.V. All rights reserved. Published in the United States by Golden Books, an imprint of Random House Children's Books, a division of Penguin Random House LLC, 1745 Broadway, New York, NY 10019, and in Canada by Penguin Random House Canada Limited, Toronto. Originally published as three separate titles by Golden Books as *Follow the Ninja!* and *Green vs. Mean* in 2015 and *Frog Fight!* in 2016. Golden Books, A Golden Book, A Little Golden Book, the G colophon, and the distinctive gold spine are registered trademarks of Penguin Random House LLC. Nickelodeon, Teenage Mutant Ninja Turtles, and all related titles, logos, and characters are trademarks of Viacom International Inc. and Viacom Overseas Holdings C.V. Based on characters created by Peter Laird and Kevin Eastman.
T: 472144
ISBN 978-0-399-55359-2
randomhousekids.com
MANUFACTURED IN CHINA
10 9 8 7 6 5 4 3 2 1

Many years ago, a strange chemical turned four regular turtles into powerful mutants. Now they live in a secret hideaway deep beneath the streets of New York City.

They're strong.

They're brothers.

They're always ready for adventure.

They're the Teenage Mutant Ninja Turtles!

Leonardo is the leader. He's serious, and he's dedicated to his martial arts studies.

Donatello is a brilliant inventor. He can build anything from parts he finds in the sewers.

Raphael is the toughest Turtle. He's lean, green, and ready for battle.

Michelangelo is the youngest. He's always ready to pull a prank or tell a joke.

The Turtles' underground lair is an awesome hangout where they watch television, play video games, and even skateboard.

Splinter was once a man, but he mutated . . .
into a giant rat. Now he teaches the Turtles the ways
of the ninja. The Turtles train hard and learn about
offensive attacks, defensive poses, and sneaking
through the shadows.

But mainly they learn that it's really hard to be a ninja.

Sometimes the Turtles sneak out of their secret lair at night and visit the streets of New York.

"Remember, guys, we can't be seen," Leonardo says. "Four giant turtles might freak people out."

The city is busy and
exciting. It's filled with
action, adventure, and
best of all . . . PIZZA!

But the Turtles must be careful, because the city is also full of fearsome foes.

The Kraang are invaders from another dimension who want to take over the planet Earth. They are fleshy pink aliens that live inside robots called Kraang-droids. The Kraang-droids can disguise themselves to look just like humans! They made the strange chemical that mutated Splinter and the Turtles.

Shredder, the most powerful martial arts master in the world, commands a fierce army of ninjas called the Foot Clan. He is an old enemy of the Turtles' teacher, Splinter. Shredder has vowed to destroy Splinter and the Turtles.

Xever was a master criminal until he was
exposed to the mutagen made by the Kraang.
Now he is Fishface, a giant fishlike creature with
a poisonous bite. A scientist built him robot legs,
so he can run on land.

While searching for the Turtles, ninja master
Chris Bradford was also splashed with mutagen.
He became a powerful half-man, half-dog creature
called Dogpound. He's fiercely loyal to his martial
arts master, Shredder.

The Turtles are not alone in their battles against the bad guys. A teenage girl named April O'Neil helps them. April's father is a great scientist who has been captured by the Kraang, and she is on a mission to find him.

Wherever there is evil, Leonardo, Donatello, Raphael, and Michelangelo will be there to stop it.

"Time to bash some bots!" yells Raphael.

After their battles, the Turtles return to the safety of their lair to celebrate.

"Ahh," sighs Michelangelo. "Victory tastes like pizza."

Turtle power!

TEENAGE MUTANT NINJA
TURTLES

FOLLOW THE NINJA!

The Teenage Mutant Ninja Turtles were on patrol. They had been looking for mutagen containers all night, but they hadn't found any.

"I'm so bored," Mikey whined.

"Let's take a break and do something fun,"
suggested Leo, the Turtles' leader.
"Awesome!" his brothers cheered.

"It's time for a training session!" Leo exclaimed.
"Aww," Raph, Donnie, and Mikey moaned. Ninja
exercises didn't sound like fun to them.

Leo had an idea
to make training exciting.
"We'll play King of the Mountain,"
he said, jumping to the top of Dragon
Gate. "I'll stand up here, and you
try to get past me using ninja skills."

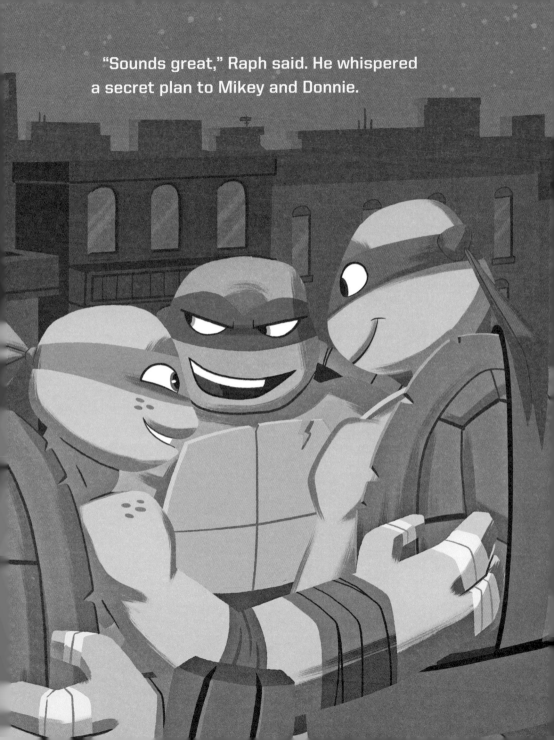

"Sounds great," Raph said. He whispered
a secret plan to Mikey and Donnie.

Mikey went first. He put on his headphones,
then flipped, spun, and danced right past Leo.
"Ninjas don't do that!" Leo protested.

Donnie calculated a sneaky way to throw his ninja stars. They bounced and skipped off buildings—right toward Leo.

Leo ducked, and when he looked up, Donnie was behind him.

$$2ab+b^2$$

$$\frac{b}{a+b}$$

$$(a+b)^2$$

$$\frac{5x}{2}$$

Raph threw his *sai* straight at Leo.
As Leo dodged it, Raph jumped past him.
"That's not fair!" Leo shouted.

Leo was really mad. "You guys never take my orders seriously."

"Well, you always want us to fight just like you," Raph replied as he, Donnie, and Mikey marched away.

Back at the lair, Leo spoke to his teacher, Splinter. "Maybe I'm not cut out to be a leader," he said.

"A true ninja must be unpredictable," Splinter said. "And a true leader doesn't always tell his followers what to do.

He must trust them to grow on their own."

The next night, the Turtles went out again. Suddenly, Karai jumped from the shadows. She was a very dangerous ninja—and she wasn't alone. An army of ninja robots stood behind her!

"My Footbots are programmed to know every ninja move," she said. "You can't beat them!"

Karai commanded the Footbots to capture the Turtles. The bots charged, and the battle began. The Footbots ducked the Turtles' punches. They blocked the Turtles' kicks. The Turtles couldn't stop them!

Leo was sure the Turtles would lose this fight . . . until he remembered Splinter's words: *A true ninja must be unpredictable.*

"You can't program a ninja," Leo said. Then he yelled to his brothers. "Do you remember King of the Mountain? Show these bots your original ninja moves!"

The Footbots weren't programmed to deal with Mikey's dancing.
Donnie was too sneaky for them.
And Raph's power put the bots on the run!

"That's the most fun I've ever had following your orders!" Raph exclaimed.

"That's the most fun I've had giving them," Leo replied.

Mikey threw a smoke bomb, and the Turtles vanished into a purple cloud.

Back at their lair, the Turtles were ready to relax.

"Who wants to play King of the Mountain?" Leo joked.

"I'd rather play Follow the Leader," Raph said with a smile.

Leo, Donnie, and Raph were mad. Mikey had wrecked the living room in April's farmhouse—again!

"Mikey, what have you done?" yelled Leo.

Mikey gulped. "Ice Cream Kitty and I were . . . studying barbarian fighting techniques?"

"Some ninja you are!" Raph sneered.

After his brothers left, Mikey packed a
bag and took off. "I'm not going to stay
where I'm not wanted," he said sadly.

In the woods, a really big frog jumped onto Mikey's head!

"Stop it!" Mikey cried, tossing the frog with a karate throw.

"Gosh!" The frog got up and brushed himself off. "I'm Napoleon Bonafrog, the greatest warrior anyone's ever seen. Will you teach me your totally sweet ninja moves?"

Mikey showed Napoleon his flying
ninja kick.

Then Napoleon showed Mikey *his* sweet
move—catching flies. "C'mon," he told his new
friend. "I'll take you to my home."

Napoleon took Mikey to a frog fortress high up in a tree.

When the frog leader, Attila, heard that Mikey had run away from his brothers and some humans, he invited the Turtle to stay.

Humans had driven Attila and his frogs from their home. The frog king thought Mikey had also lost his home to humans.

That night, Attila ordered his frog soldiers to march to a nearby farmhouse. It was April's house!

April, Casey, and the Turtles were searching
for Mikey when the frog soldiers attacked.

The frog soldiers wrapped their sticky tongues around April and Casey. They dragged them back to the fortress and threw them into cages!

"What are you doing to my friends?" cried Mikey.

"*Friends?*" Attila frowned. "I thought you said these humans were terrible!"

Mikey scratched his head. "Well, that's not exactly true."

"Side with humans, suffer with humans!" shouted Attila.

As frog soldiers threw Mikey into a cage, three shadows dropped down. The other Turtles had followed Casey and April—and were ready for a frog fight!

The Turtles fought hard . . .

but they were outnumbered and losing . . .

until Napoleon joined in with a mighty ninja kick!

"Sweet moves, Napoleon!" said Mikey as the frog leaped up and unlocked his cage.

"I learned them from the second-best ninja ever," Napoleon replied with a grin.

Mikey freed April and Casey as a burning
branch fell onto the fortress.

"We must totally flee!" Napoleon cried.
"Follow me!"

"No! Stand and fight against the humans!" shouted Attila.

Casey had to prove that humans weren't all bad—and fast! "Don't take this the wrong way, buddy," he said as he whacked the frog king over the head.

Casey and April carried Attila safely
away from the burning fortress.

"Humans saved me?" Attila marveled when he woke.

April nodded. "Not all humans are bad. And I'd like to believe that not all mutant frogs are bad, either."

"Perhaps there's a world where frogs, turtles, and revolting humans can live together in harmony," said Attila.

Attila told the frog soldiers to line up behind their new general—Napoleon! "You showed wisdom with these Turtles and humans," Attila told Napoleon proudly.

"Where are you going to go?" Mikey asked Napoleon.

"South. We'll find a new home there." Napoleon hopped to the front of the frog army. "Goodbye, Mikey!"

"There goes one brave frog," Mikey sighed.

"It's good to have you back, bro," said Raph.
Mikey hugged his brothers. "It's good to be
back," he said happily, and they all headed home.